Published by LionSky Publishing

Text Copyright (c) 2015 by Cerece Rennie Murphy

Image Copyright (c) 2015 by Greg Garay

Illustration by Greg Garay

Cover & Interior design by Greg Garay

Printed in the United States of America

ISBN 13: 978-0-9856210-5-6

Library of Congress Control Number:

LionSky
PUBLISHING

# Ellis AND The Magic Mirror

Story by Cerece and Aryeh Rennie Murphy
Illustration by Greg Garay

# CHAPTER 1
# EARTH DAY

**E**llis Monroe couldn't wait to get to school! It was Earth Week at Harriett Tubman Elementary School, and every day they were going to learn something new about Planet Earth - from the forests and trees of the Amazon to the way people lived thousands of years ago.

Ellis and his little sister Freddye ate their breakfast as fast as they could and ran out the door to meet their friend, Toro Quispe, so that they could walk to school together.

"Hi, Toro," Ellis called to his best friend who was waiting for him at the corner. "Can you believe it's Earth Week?"

"Yeah, I know," Toro said excitedly. "My mom is coming on Thursday to talk about all the different kinds of plants there are and why we need to save them."

"Cool!" Ellis replied. He wasn't quite sure what Toro's Mom did, but he knew she was a doctor like his Dad and travelled all over the world. She also made the best brownies ever.

"My Dad is coming to our class on Friday to talk about all the cool stuff you can find as an archeologist. He's going to bring his whole collection of artifacts. Aren't you, Dad?" Ellis asked.

Before Dr. Monroe could reply, Freddye chimed in. "But Daddy's coming to my class first. Right, Daddy?" Freddye added proudly.

Dr. Monroe chuckled.

"Yes, Freddye. On Friday, I'm coming to your class first, with as many artifacts as the museum will let me carry."

They all agreed that would be awesome.

The crowd of children and parents grew as they crossed the street carefully and walked into the schoolyard.

"Thanks, Dad!" Ellis said. Dr. Monroe gave them all one big hug before letting them run into school.

Once inside, Ellis' teacher, Ms. Lee, let them know that Earth Week wasn't the only special event happening at their school. They had a new student named Buddy Cruster.

Everyone was nice to Buddy as they went through the first day of Earth Week. They included Buddy in their activities as they made paper models of the globe and found all the countries on Ms. Lee's large map of the world.

1

But though he seemed happy at first, as the day went on, Buddy got more and more grumpy. In fact, Buddy complained about almost everything. He didn't want to learn the names of the different countries. He didn't want to make his own globe. He didn't seem to want to learn, and he didn't want anyone else to either. By the time the bell rang for lunch, Buddy had already been sent to the quiet desk for trying to distract other children from their work.

Ellis thought his behavior was strange, but figured maybe Buddy was just nervous about being in a new school. Ellis was so excited about Earth Week that he felt sure that if he just worked harder to help, Buddy would like it, too.

After lunch, Ellis tried to tell Buddy about all the cool things they would be learning throughout the week, but Buddy just laughed and rolled his eyes. By the end of the day, Ellis felt sad that Buddy wasn't enjoying any of the things he thought were so great and it made him less excited about Earth Week, too.

At the dinner table that night, his parents could tell that Ellis was not as excited about his day as they had expected.

"How was your day?" his Dad asked while they ate dinner together.

"It was okay, I guess."

"Didn't the Earth Week celebration start today?" his mother asked. "You were so excited this morning about all the things you were going to do. What happened?"

"Well… it was pretty cool today and I did have fun, except this new kid in my class kept saying how school was dumb. At first I tried to help him, and then I tried to ignore him, but I guess I just wanted everyone to be as excited about Earth Week as I am."

"I understand," his Dad said, reaching out to comfort him. "Not everyone is going to be excited about the same things that you are, but don't let anyone ruin your good time, okay?"

Ellis nodded, knowing his Dad was right. After a moment, his father added, "Besides, I think I have something that will cheer you up."

"Really! What is it?" Ellis's eyes gleamed with excitement. Slowly, his father reached behind his chair and pulled out a package wrapped in a soft brown cloth. His sister Freddye moved closer to get a better look while Ellis watched his father place the package on the kitchen table and carefully pull back the cloth.

Inside was a strange and beautiful object made of very old, tarnished metal and glass.

"Can I touch it?" Ellis asked his father as he reached out his hands.

"Okay," Ellis' Dad replied, "but you must be very careful."

"Cool!" Ellis exclaimed as he picked up the handle and held it high. "It's a mirror," he said, looking at the faint shimmer of his own reflection in the glass.

"More of a looking glass, actually," his father replied. "Ancient legend says that if you focus the lens on a person or anything you want to understand, it will show you the truth of what that thing really is. In some ancient cultures, it is called a heart mirror."

"What do you mean, Daddy?" Freddye asked.

"That means it can show you if someone is truly good or truly bad. Look and see for yourself."

Dr. Monroe showed Ellis and Freddye how to point the mirror right at him. At first, Freddye and Ellis could only see their own reflections in the glass, but then slowly their reflection faded and the image of their father became clear. In the looking glass, his whole body was surrounded with a strange deep orange light that made them happy.

"What do you see?" their father asked.

"That you have a good heart, Daddy," Freddye answered while Ellis stared in amazement.

"Well, that's good to know," their Dad said with a laugh. Ellis noticed some strange markings around the edges of the mirror just as his mother was calling them upstairs for bath time.

"What do these marks mean, Dad? Can you read them?"

"That's a great question, Ellis, but no, I can't."

"I wish I could," Ellis said, still staring at the mirror. "I want to know what it says.

Can we keep it, Dad? Pleassseee?"

"I'm afraid not, but I'll have it with me for a few days," he said thoughtfully. "I need to make a rubbing of the marks and send them to a professor who can help me read them. But after that, I have to bring it to the museum to be kept and studied with all the other artifacts."

"OK," Ellis said, but he was only half-listening as he placed the mirror back down on the cloth. He couldn't wait to take it to school tomorrow and show Toro what his Dad had found.

# CHAPTER 2
# A SURPRISE

**W**hen Ellis began school the next day, Buddy was still there complaining and whining, but Ellis didn't pay him any attention. In fact, he had a hard time paying attention to anything, because in his book bag Ellis was hiding something special–the mirror his father showed him last night. He couldn't wait to take it out and show Toro when they met underneath their favorite tree at recess.

After what seemed to take FOREVER, the class bell finally rang. It was time to go outside. By the time Ellis made it to their tree, Toro was waiting for him.

"Hey, Ellis!" Toro said with a smile. "Why did you bring your book bag? I thought we were going to play tag."

"Not today," Ellis grinned, laying the bag down carefully. "I have a surprise to show you."

Ellis pulled the mirror out of his backpack and held it up for Toro to see.

"Cool mirror!" Toro said. "Where did you find it?"

"I didn't. My dad found it. And it's not a mirror. It's magic!"

Toro's eyes opened wide with surprise.

"How do you know?" Toro asked.

"Look," Ellis said, holding the mirror out to him.

Toro took the mirror and looked around. First, he pointed the mirror at the forest behind their school. Slowly his reflection faded away so that he could see the trees in front of him glowing with green yellow light.

"Wow… How does it do that?" Toro asked.

"My Dad says it's a heart mirror. It shows you the good and the bad in the people and things around you. It shows you what's really inside of them."

Together, they sat under the tree testing everything around them. Toro was not surprised that his best friend Ellis beamed brilliantly with a purple yellow glow that matched his smile. Toro's glow was blue and yellow but just as bright. As they scanned the playground, they saw that most of the children in the school had soft glows of their own in almost every color of the rainbow. Some lights shone brighter than others, but they all glowed.

With five minutes left before the lunch bell, Ellis and Toro gave themselves one last look around the playground before they would have to put the looking glass away and prepare for lunch. But just as they thought they were finished, something made them both jump.

At the edge of the playground, sitting alone on a bench sat a bumpy, lumpy sour-faced troll. The fact that the children nearest to the bench didn't seem to notice him at all was very strange. Ellis and Toro wanted to yell out and warn everyone, but for a moment they were too stunned to speak.

"What is that?" Toro asked Ellis.

"Who is that?" Ellis answered, remembering that the looking glass showed the inside of a person. The outside could only be seen with the naked eye.

As if realizing the same thought at the same time, Ellis and Toro lowered the looking glass together and, as they did, the image of the troll slowly dissolved to reveal Buddy Cruster on the bench, staring back at them with a scowl on his face.

# CHAPTER 3
# SPECIAL

**S**uddenly, the lunch bell rang. Ellis and Toro watched Buddy hurry off with the same sour expression the troll wore on his face.

"We need to tell our teachers," Toro said as he got to his feet.

"Maybe," Ellis replied, putting the looking glass into his backpack. "But who's going to believe us if we tell them there's a troll in our school?"

"What if we just showed them the mirror?" Toro replied.

"I'm not even supposed to have the mirror," Ellis reminded him. "If my Dad finds out that I took it out of the house, I'm going to be in BIG trouble."

Toro and Ellis were silent for a moment as they considered exactly how much trouble they would be in if they shared the fact that they had the mirror with anyone.

"I wonder what he's doing here in the first place," Toro asked aloud. "All he ever does is complain about school."

Ellis' eyes lit up.

"That's it, Toro! We need to find out why a troll who hates school is hanging around here."

Toro looked doubtful. "How are we supposed to do that?"

"We'll follow him after school and see where he comes from. Maybe then we can figure out why he's hiding out here."

"I don't know, Ellis…"

"Come on, Toro! No one else knows who Buddy really is. I'm going to have to give back this mirror soon anyway. If we don't find out what's going on now, then we'll never know."

Toro looked towards the door where Buddy had gone into lunch. Ellis' plan made him nervous, but more than anything, he was curious.

"Okay," Toro said looking back at Ellis, "but just this once."

Ellis, Toro, and Freddye met behind the school as they always did. Buddy was in the Principal's office – in trouble for not listening in art class. While they waited for Buddy to come out, Toro and Ellis explained to Freddye what the mirror had shown them about Buddy and what they planned to do.

To Ellis' surprise, his sister seemed to think following Buddy was a good idea.

"I saw him in the lunch room throwing food in people's hair. He's not nice," Freddye huffed as she tightened the laces on her high tops.

When Buddy finally came out of the Principal's office, he was smiling, even though he'd just gotten in trouble.

"Yeah, that was cool," he laughed giving the two other boys who'd gotten in trouble with him high-fives. "Let's do it again, tomorrow."

But the other two boys didn't look so happy.

"Aren't you worried about what your parents will say? I know my parents are going to be so mad when they hear this," one of the boys said.

"Nah," Buddy said, shrugging his shoulders. "And even if they were mad, so what? Who cares, right?"

The two boys waved goodbye and shook their heads, more than a little surprised that Buddy didn't seem to care about anything.

When Buddy finally left, he took the path behind their school that led into the woods. Ellis, Toro and Freddye followed him from a safe distance, using the looking glass as their guide.

At first it seemed that Buddy was alone. But then, Ellis, Freddye, and Toro began to see other children coming from different paths in the woods. To their surprise, they all seemed to be going in the same direction as Buddy.

Ellis, Freddye, and Toro stopped for a moment and moved the looking glass around to see each child on the path clearly. Their mouths hung open as they realized that each child was a troll.

They hid behind a bush as all the trolls gathered at a clearing in the middle of the forest and began to talk. The shortest troll, who stood in the center of the group, spoke first.

"How many did we get today?" he roared.

"Four in detention," one troll said.

"I got one child suspended for fighting," another shouted.

"Three won't do their homework tonight," one more yelled out. All the trolls laughed happily.

"Good, Good!" the shortest one said. "We have to keep them from doing their best or one day they will be smart enough to find us and we can't let that happen. We can't let them learn!"

The group of trolls clapped and cheered so loudly that the sound frightened Ellis, Toro and Freddye. But the short one quieted them all down again just before

turning to Buddy.

"And you, Buddy, who did you stop from learning today?"

"I got two boys called into the Principal's office," Buddy answered quietly.

"Yes, very good… and Ellis?" The troll asked.

All three children held their breath when they heard Ellis' name.

"He didn't pay any attention to me. I couldn't get him into trouble." Buddy held his head low as he told the group.

The short troll frowned. "And you're sure he is the one? You saw the mark?"

"Yes, I saw it on the back of his hand. It was just as you described," Buddy answered.

"He has the birthmark in the shape of a star."

The short troll's frown deepened. "Then you must try harder. Now that we know he is the Stone Keeper, we must stop Ellis from learning. He's just too curious. If he gets the stones, he will have the power to awaken the others and stop our plans."

Buddy, along with the other trolls, nodded their heads in agreement.

"We must stop Ellis!" they cried as they moved deeper into the forest and out of sight.

When the trolls were far enough away, Freddye, Toro, and Ellis finally let out the breath they had been holding. With just enough light left from the sun to find their way back, the children were happy to leave the forest and began walking home.

"What's a stone keeper?" Freddye asked, fighting to keep the tears from her eyes.

The things they said about her brother scared her.

"I don't know," Toro answered, "but if it means Ellis is in danger, then we have to do something."

They waited for Ellis to respond, but he was deep in thought as he stared at the birthmark on his left hand. Even though he knew his family and friends loved him, Ellis had never thought of himself as someone special before, someone with the "power to awaken others."

"I don't know what it means either," Ellis finally admitted, "but we better get home. Toro, I'll send you a message tonight."

By the time Ellis and Freddye made it home, their mother told them that their father had to travel to New York City to help a professor date some artifacts he'd found near the Genghis River in India.

Ellis tried not to let his relief show as he realized he'd have one more day before he had to return the looking glass back to his father's desk.

Both Freddye and Ellis were unusually quiet during their homework and dinner. At first their mother thought it was just because they missed their father, who almost always ate with them, but by the time they were dressed for bed, she was worried.

"Your father promised to be home in time to make his presentation in both your classes on Friday, so don't worry," she said, trying to reassure them.

"We know," Freddye replied. "We're not worried about that."

"Then is there something else you're worried about?" their mother asked gently.

"You both have been very quiet tonight. You know, you can always talk to me."

After a moment of silence, Ellis finally asked his mother what he'd been thinking about all evening.

"Mom, do you think I'm special? I mean, really special?"

Understanding how serious his question was, Mrs. Monroe took a moment to step back and look at each of her children.

"The truth is, Ellis, that we are all special in our own way. A way that is unique to each person on the earth. Sometimes our gifts seem small, other times they seem too big even for us to believe. But we all have a purpose that is important.

"But in all my life, I've never met two people like you. Ellis, you're curious, smart and brave in a way that makes people want to follow you wherever you lead them. And you, Freddye, are one of the smartest, most fearless people I've ever met. Each of you has the kind of gifts that make the world a better place.

"So yes, Ellis, you are special, very special. And so are you, Freddye."

And with that, their mother kissed them good night and closed the door. Freddye fell asleep almost immediately, still smiling from her mother's words, but Ellis was up and more sure of what he needed to do than ever.

He wrote a quick note to Toro, put it in a glass bottle, sealed the cap over it, and hooked it to the rope that looped from Toro's house to his. He pulled the rope carrying the glass along until he heard it tap the side of Toro's house.

When Toro heard the sound on his windowsill, he threw up the sash and smiled. After reading the note inside, Toro took his flashlight and used the three flash "Yes" signal that he and Ellis had created to send his reply. Toro was so excited that he read the note one more time before heading off to bed.

It read:

***One day left with the looking glass. Back to the woods tomorrow to stop whatever they have planned. Bring your bike. – Ellis***

# CHAPTER 4
# INTO THE WOODS

**E**llis woke up the next morning ready to go. In his book bag, he packed everything he could think of to help him face the trolls. He had his notebook, his nun chucks, the magic mirror, and his trusty stuffed penguin named Chirpy, just in case. It always made him feel better when Chirpy was around.

His sister, Freddye, packed a few extra things in her book bag, too, including her wooden sword from fencing class, her special headlight that fit on top of her head, and a fresh pack of glow worms just in case they got lost and needed to find their way home in the dark.

"Your book bags look pretty full today," their Mom said when they came downstairs for breakfast.

"We're just bringing some extra supplies for a special project we're working on," Ellis replied.

"Okay," Mrs. Monroe said, looking at them curiously as she poured warm milk into their cups.

"Well your Dad called this morning and wanted to let you know that his friend in New York was able to read the carvings on the mirror handle he showed you the other night. It says 'May the light inside protect you from the things you see.'"

When Ellis and Freddye's eyes widened in surprise, their Mom chuckled.

"He knew you'd be excited to find out what it said, so he made me promise to tell you before you went off to school today."

Ellis and Freddye looked at each other, wondering what the words really meant, but they didn't dare ask their mother, just in case she started asking questions about the mirror and what they were doing.

"Thanks, Mom," they said quickly before finishing their breakfast in silence. Once they were done, their mother stood up from the table.

"So are we walking today or taking the car?

"Skateboard," Ellis replied, while Freddye fastened her helmet onto her head and added "Scooter."

"Wow," their mother said. "Seems like you guys are in a hurry."

Ellis just smiled. "Today, Mom, we don't want to miss a thing."

They met Toro and his mother, Mrs. Quispe, at the end of the block. Toro was on his bike. Together, the children raced to school quicker than their Moms could ever remember them doing before.

"What's gotten into them?" Toro's mom wondered as the two women watched their kids go through the school doors.

"Who knows," Ellis and Freddye's mom laughed, "but it's good to see them excited about school."

For most of the day, it was hard for Ellis to focus on his schoolwork. Buddy was constantly trying to talk to him, make jokes or ask a question, but Ellis just ignored him. Besides, Ellis noticed that most of Buddy's jokes weren't funny at all. They were just mean things you shouldn't say about other people. When Ellis kept ignoring him, Buddy turned his attention on other students. In a way, that made it worse.

Every time Ellis saw Buddy trying to distract another classmate, it made him want to stand up and yell "Cut it out!" but then he knew he would be the one to get in trouble and that was just what Buddy wanted.

So Ellis tried even harder to make sure he did his best, but it still felt like a very long day.

When school was finally over, Ellis, Freddye, and Toro met at the school playground and waited for Buddy, who was in the Principal's office - again.

Their plan was to follow Buddy into the woods until they found the place where all the trolls lived. From there, they would try to find out why the trolls thought children going to school and learning was so terrible.

Things started out well enough. Ellis, Toro, and Freddye followed Buddy down the same path he walked the day before. And just like yesterday, more trolls came. But instead of stopping to talk, they kept walking deeper and deeper into the woods.

The deeper they went, the more the tall trees blocked the sunlight. Freddye was glad that she'd brought her glowworms. She began dropping them along the dark path that led farther into the forest than they'd ever been.

Toro and Ellis also reached into their bags to get things they thought could help them on their journey. Toro brought out his compass, while Ellis held the mirror in front, so that nothing would get past them.

They walked for a while behind the group of trolls until they came to the biggest tree any of the children had ever seen. While every other tree in the forest rustled with green leaves, this one stood without a single leaf on its branches. The whole tree was covered in a green-black moss that made the tree look heavy and sad. Near the roots of the tree was a deep dark hole that looked like the entrance to a cave. A big sign beside the hole read "Enter Bugabols".

As the trolls began to step inside the cave, Toro, Freddye, and Ellis hid behind a bush.

There were so many trolls that Ellis and Toro stopped counting after one hundred. In fact, there were so many that they couldn't see Buddy anywhere.

"What are we going to do? There are too many of them," Freddye asked as quietly as she could.

"Let's wait until they all go inside, then maybe we can follow them," Ellis replied.

Toro nodded as he continued to watch the trolls disappear into the tree.

"Where is Buddy?" he whispered suddenly. Though Toro had been looking for him, he still hadn't seen Buddy go into the tree. Each of them turned to look around and that's when it happened. A small branch snapped underneath them.

In the quiet of the forest, the noise was as loud as any noise could be and the five trolls who were still standing at the mouth of the cave turned in their direction.

Ellis, Toro, and Freddye froze in their hiding place, but it was too late.

All of a sudden, Buddy jumped out of the forest from behind them. Ellis, Toro, and Freddye screamed in surprise and sprang to their feet to get away.

"There they are!" Buddy cried as he forced them out into the open with six pairs of troll eyes looking right at them.

# CHAPTER 5
# STONEKEEPER

**T**he shortest troll, the same one that the children had seen the day before, stepped towards them with an angry look on his face.

"Why have you followed us?" he asked in a child's voice. "We're just children playing in the woods."

But with his mirror held high, Ellis was not fooled.

"You're no child," Ellis answered, stepping in front of his sister and Toro.

"You're… a troll. We can see who you really are!"

Those behind the shortest troll gasped loudly, but he silenced them all with a wave of his hand.

"We are no trolls! I am Mal and we are Bugabols! How are you able to see our true forms? Who are you?"

"He is Ellis Monroe, the Stone Keeper," Buddy answered as he came to stand beside Mal. The other Bugabols echoed Buddy's words. Their eyes narrowed as they looked at the children.

"It doesn't matter how I can see you," Ellis replied. "What matters is we know who you are and we want to know why you want to stop us from learning?"

Ellis could see from the corner of his eye that Toro and Freddye had stepped closer to him. On his right, Freddye had her sword out and her flashlight on her head. Her eyebrows were drawn together in determination to face whatever came their way. To his left, Toro stood tall with his bow and plunger arrow in his hand, pulled back and ready to fire. Ellis also saw that Toro's book bag was open and filled to the brim with more arrows. Ellis pulled his nun chucks from his book bag while holding the mirror firmly in his left hand.

Together they formed a tight crescent of protection for each other.

Mal stepped closer.

"We must stop the children from learning so that they will not grow to discover our secret. We must live in darkness, and children bring light to the darkness. And you, Ellis Monroe, have the power to awaken the others. Because of you, the children will bring a light that will end the darkness. Which is why, now that you know who we are, we can not let you and your friends leave."

As soon as Mal finished speaking, the trolls began moving towards them with large stones and pointed sticks in their hands.

"If we stay together, we can make it," Toro whispered.

"We just need to keep them in front of us so that we can make our way back

through the path," Freddye answered back.

"Stick together. Head towards the path – that's our plan," Ellis agreed.

Before they could say another word, the Bugabols were on them. From the front, Buddy lunged toward Ellis with a broken branch. To Ellis' left, Mal sneered while holding a metal-tipped spear in both hands. In a flash, Ellis swung his nun chucks at the closest troll to him, knocking Buddy to the ground. Then, Ellis turned left, extending his nun chucks out. With the first strike, Ellis wrapped the chain of his nun chucks around the metal tip of Mal's spear and pulled it out of the troll's hands. He barely had time to toss it aside before he saw Mal pick up a large rock on the ground. Ellis spun away quickly before the troll could take aim. Then Ellis swung down, catching the troll at the wrist and knocking the rock out of his hand. With his next swing, Ellis angled upwards, hitting Mal in the chin. With a heavy thud, Mal landed flat on his back. As Buddy and Mal struggled to get back on their feet, Ellis tried to prepare himself for their next attack. But to his surprise, when they did get up, they just ran away, like all bullies do.

Next, Freddye used her sword to drive back a troll who was trying to sneak up on them from behind. Though he held a long sharp stick in each hand, Freddye knew how to use her sword to fight off his attacks. They circled each other as Freddye swung her sword hard and fast until she finally broke both of his sticks in two. Frightened by her skill and strength, the Bugabol turned and escaped into the forest.

While Ellis and Freddye moved around to fight off the Bugabols, Toro stood his ground, using his plungers to knock the three remaining trolls down one by one. It took the trolls quite awhile to remove the plungers from their faces, but once they got up, like the others, they chose to retreat into the trees.

"Where are the others?" Freddye asked, breathing heavily.

Suddenly, Ellis, Toro, and Freddye felt the ground shake, just before a group of Bugabols poured out from the hole in the tree. On each side of them, more Bugabols came up from underground doors, hidden in the dirt. Within a few short moments, they were surrounded.

"Go!" Ellis shouted as they all turned to run.

Freddye with her head flashlight and Toro with his compass led the way, searching for glowworms on the ground as they ran. They knew they needed to keep to the path that had led them to this place or they would be lost.

From just behind them, Ellis kept a close watch on the Bugabols. It looked like every troll they had followed into the forest was after them.

More than once, Ellis had to swing his nun chucks to keep a Bugabol from grabbing his backpack and pulling him down. Toro shot plunger arrows to their right when a few trolls got too close. To their left, Freddye swung her sword out to stop trolls from reaching out and grabbing her.

They were running as hard as they could, but in his heart Ellis feared that they

would never be able to run fast enough to outrun them all.

Up ahead he could see the clearing where the trolls had gathered the day before. It stood before them like a beacon with a single ray of sunlight shining through.

Suddenly, Ellis understood the meaning of the words carved onto the mirror handle. May the light inside protect you from the things you see.

"Head to the clearing!" Ellis shouted. "Hurry!"

They pushed themselves as fast as their feet could fly until they made it into the clearing with the Bugabols trailing just behind.

But instead of running through the clearing, Ellis stepped into the Sun and turned around so that its light surrounded him. He held the mirror high into the air and noticed that the birthmark on his hand began to glow. Slowly, the looking glass began to turn back into a shiny mirror.

Instantly, the Sun's rays bounced off the mirror and cover the dark forest with a sparkling bright light.

The Bugabols stood frozen in fear as the beauty of the light touched each of them and turned them all to stone. Just then, a gust of air blew through the forest and the children watched with wide eyes as each stone troll crumbled to dust in the wind.

When it was over, a woman's voice rang out from the fading light.

"Well done, Stonekeeper!" the voice said in a tone that was gentle and kind. "All true power begins with the light inside you. May you, Freddye, and Toro continue to learn and grow so that you may become strong in wisdom. For the journey of the Stonekeeper has just begun."

"Who are you?" Ellis called out as Freddye and Toro stepped into the sun's light with him.

"Yeah, and how do you know our names?" Freddye added suspiciously.

"We were sent to watch over you," the voice replied. "And to give you this."

As the sun's light faded away with the woman's voice, Freddye noticed something shining beneath the dirt at their feet.

"Ellis, look!"

Freddye bent down and picked up the beautiful purple-yellow stone that shimmered in the fading light and handed it to her brother.

Toro stared at the gem in amazement. " Wow...Stonekeeper. You did it, Ellis!" he said while patting his best friend on the back.

"We all did it. Together," Ellis replied with a shy smile.

"But what does it mean?" Freddye asked. She looked nervously across the forest where just a few minutes ago trolls had been ready to catch them.

"I don't know," Ellis replied, looking down at the stone in his hand. He was having a hard time believing anything that had just taken place. "But the lady said that we needed to continue to learn and grow on our journey. And right now, I'm thinking that means homework. It's getting late. We better get home."

With the help of Freddye's glowworms and Toro's compass, they found their way back to their scooter, skateboard, and bike and made it home safely without getting in too much trouble for being late.

Ellis and Freddye even managed to put the mirror back into their father's desk just before he got home that evening.

After homework, dinner, and bath time, their parents put Freddye and Ellis to bed like they did each day, with a story and a kiss goodnight. But everything felt brand new for Ellis, The Stonekeeper, as he fell asleep with the stone he'd been given in the forest held tightly in his hand.

~ The End ~

# ABOUT US

Aryeh is a very curious boy and Cerece is his Mommy.

We dedicate this book to boys and girls everywhere who still like lots of pictures when reading all those words.

Greg is an enthusiastic artist who loves a good story to draw.

I dedicate this book to all my nephews and nieces. If this doesn't make me the coolest uncle, I don't know what will.

To learn more about the
Ellis and The Magic Mirror series,
please visit our website at

www.theellisseries.com

CPSIA information can be obtained
at www.ICGtesting.com
Printed in the USA
LVHW012016171220
674450LV00022B/2583